MIRROR MIRROR

THE MOVIE STORYBOOK

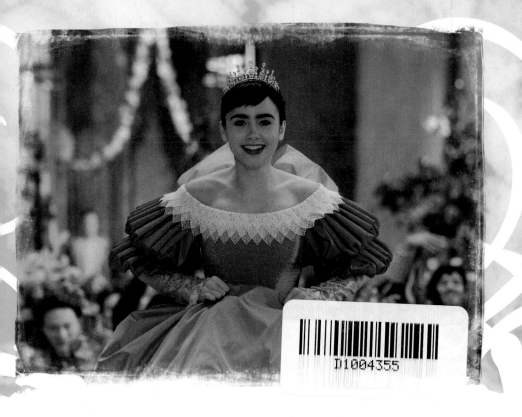

BASED ON RELATIVITY'S MOTION PICTURE
ADAPTED BY JENNE SIMON
BASED UPON THE SCREENPLAY WRITTEN BY
MELISA WALLACK AND JASON KELLER
BASED ON THE GRIMM BROTHERS' "LITTLE SNOW WHITE"
DIRECTED BY TARSEM SINGH

SCHOLASTIC INC.

New York   Toronto   London   Auckland
Sydney   Mexico City   New Delhi   Hong Kong

ISBN 978-0-545-43674-8

© 2012 Relativity Media
Published by Scholastic Inc.
SCHOLASTIC and associated logos are trademarks and/or registered trademarks of Scholastic Inc.

12 11 10 9 8 7 6 5 4 3 2 1   12 13 14 15 16 17/0

Printed in the U.S.A.   40
First printing, January 2012

nce there lived a princess named Snow White. She was good and kind, and her father, the King, loved her very much.

But the King also loved Snow White's stepmother. The beautiful Queen was jealous of the Princess. And when the King disappeared into the dark woods never to be heard from again, Snow was left to be raised by the woman who disliked her most.

Snow tried to stay out of the Queen's way. But when the Queen hosted a fancy costume ball, Snow simply had to attend. And there she was swept off her feet by a handsome prince.

As he glided Snow along the dance floor, she blushed. "I haven't danced in a long time," she said.

The Prince smiled. "Well, I intend to give you plenty of practice this evening."

Snow looked into his eyes and knew she had found her one true love.

The Queen was furious. She had decided to marry the Prince herself. "Get her out of here!" the Queen shouted to her guards.

Snow struggled as she was dragged from the castle.
The Queen smiled. "Come now, Snow," she called.
"It's important to know when you've been beaten."

Snow found herself banished to the dark
woods. She became very frightened.

And so she ran.

The forest seemed to come alive around
her. Shadows crawled along the forest floor.
Soon her fear overcame her, and she fell to
the ground.

But just when all seemed lost, seven small men came upon the Princess. They carried her home and watched over her until at last she awoke.

"The Queen sent me out here. I have nowhere to go," cried Snow.

The dwarves introduced themselves to Snow. Their names were Grimm, Butcher, Half-Pint, Chuck, Wolf, Napoleon, and Grub. The dwarves voted and decided to let Snow stay with them.

Snow continued to tell her sad story. "I've lost my father, my kingdom, and the man I love," cried Snow. "I am not strong enough to stand up to the Queen."

The dwarf named Grimm looked Snow firmly in the eye. "People say you can't be tall if you're short. That you can't be strong if you're not. But a weakness is only a weakness if you think of it that way."

Snow smiled. "Perhaps you are right."

Back at the castle, the Queen tried to make the Prince fall in love with her by slipping a love potion into his drink.

He took one sip and immediately began to roll around on the floor and nip at her heels.

The Queen was confused. She checked the potion's label.

"Puppy love?" she cried. "What am I supposed to do with a puppy?"

A few days later, the dwarves returned home from a hunt with some big news.

"Snow!" called Grimm. "You won't believe who we've caught in our trap!"

Snow came running, only to find the Prince tied up and weeping.

"Please take me back to my precious Queen! I beg you!" he cried.

Snow was stunned. Could this fool be the man she had fallen in love with?

Grimm shook his head. "He must be under some kind of spell."

"Does anyone know how to break a spell?" asked Snow.

The dwarves tried everything they could think of, but nothing worked. Until Napoleon had an idea.

"I don't know why I didn't think of it before," said Napoleon. "A kiss! The kiss of true love is always what frees someone from a spell."

And so Snow knelt down next to the Prince and closed her eyes. Softly, she whispered, "Come back to me. Please."

And then she kissed him.

Snow held her breath. Had the kiss worked?

The Prince looked deeply into Snow's eyes. "The Queen . . ."

Snow froze.

". . . is an awful, miserable woman. And Snow White is the most magical girl in the world."

As the dwarves cheered, Snow beamed with the joy of true love.

Now that Snow and the Prince were together at last, Snow marched back home and told the Queen that she was taking her rightful place on the throne.

When news spread through the Kingdom, the people rejoiced. And when the evil Queen saw that she'd lost her power over them, she fled.

The day of Snow White's wedding to the Prince was a day no one in the Kingdom would soon forget.

The King had returned from the dark woods, and happily saw his only daughter marry the man she loved.

At the reception, a strange and uninvited guest approached the bride. The frail, old woman offered Snow the gift of a shiny red apple.

"How dear of you," said Snow. But her eyes narrowed, for she recognized the Queen through her disguise.

"Age before beauty," said Snow, as she cut a slice of the surely poisoned apple and offered it to the old woman. "It's important to know when you've been beaten."

The Queen could do nothing but take a bite of the apple. After a few moments, she shrank into her robes and disappeared forever.

With that, the kingdom went back to celebrating the royal wedding.

And Snow White and her Prince lived happily ever after.